2020
Coloring
Calendar
UNICORNS & RAINBOWS

Copyright 2019 Gumdrop Press

All rights reserved.

ISBN-13: 978-1-945887-74-1

2020

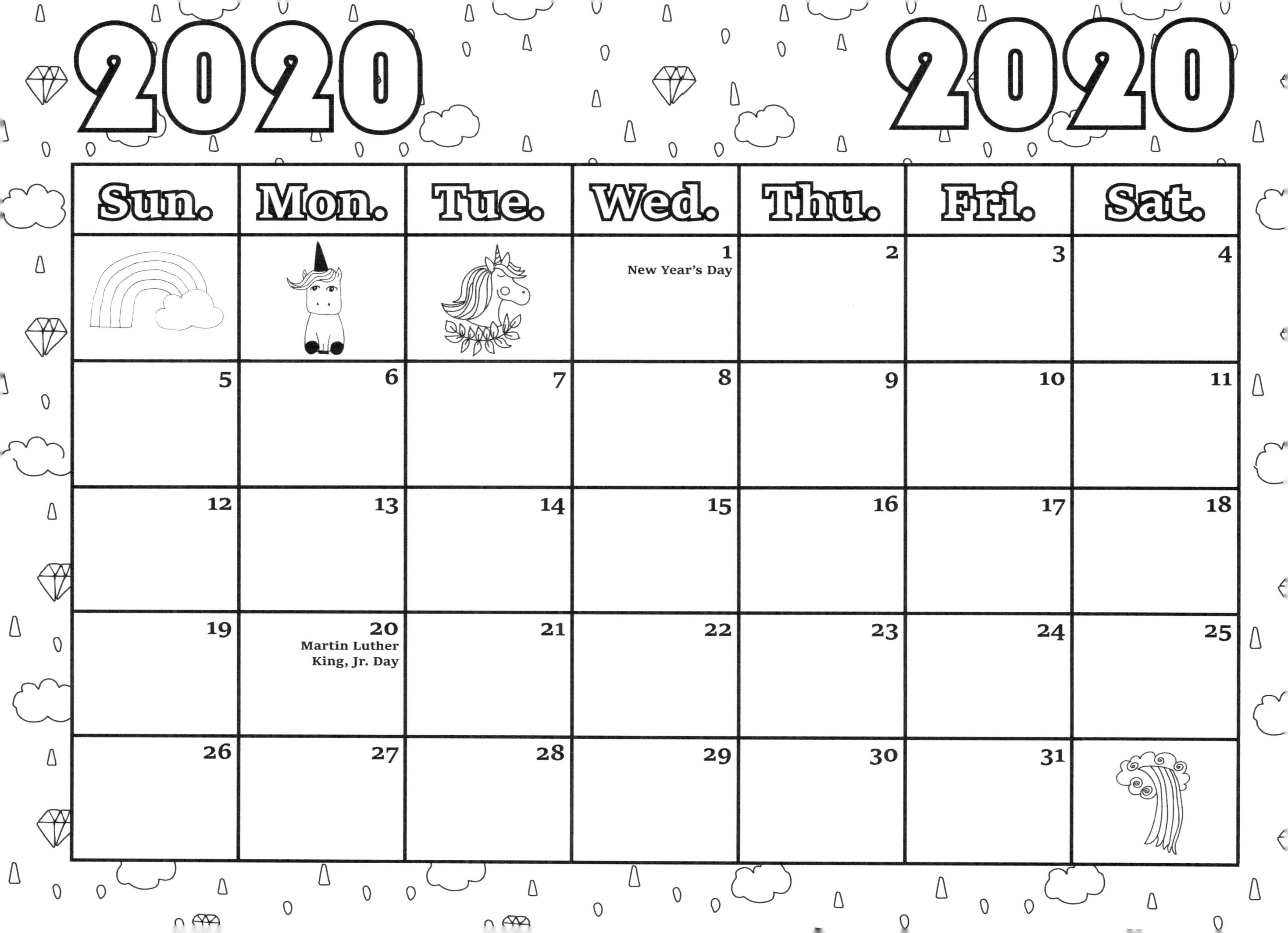

Sun.	Mon.	Tue.	Wed.	Thu.	Fri.	Sat.
			1 New Year's Day	2	3	4
5	6	7	8	9	10	11
12	13	14	15	16	17	18
19	20 Martin Luther King, Jr. Day	21	22	23	24	25
26	27	28	29	30	31	

2020

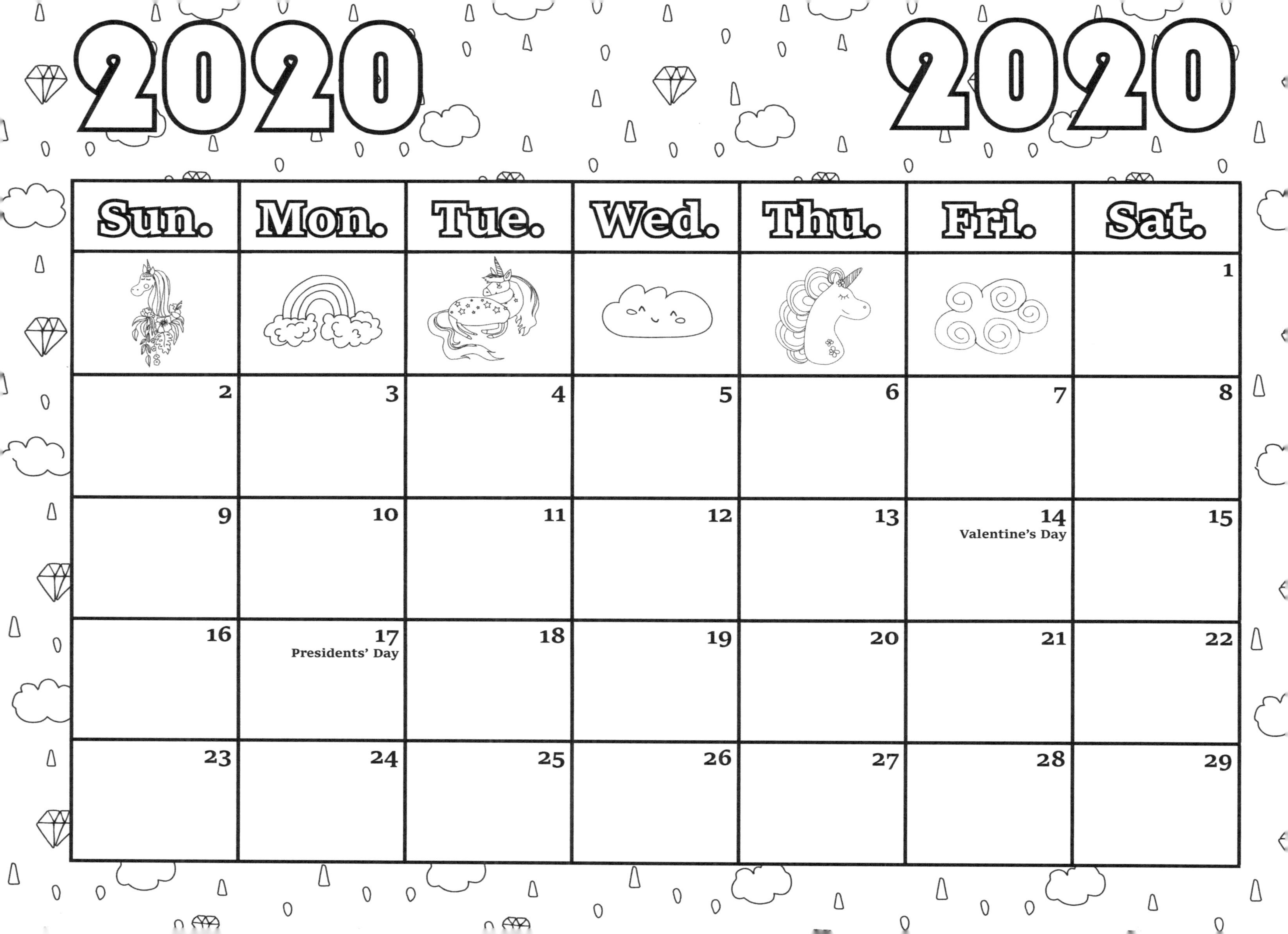

Sun.	Mon.	Tue.	Wed.	Thu.	Fri.	Sat.
						1
2	3	4	5	6	7	8
9	10	11	12	13	14 Valentine's Day	15
16	17 Presidents' Day	18	19	20	21	22
23	24	25	26	27	28	29

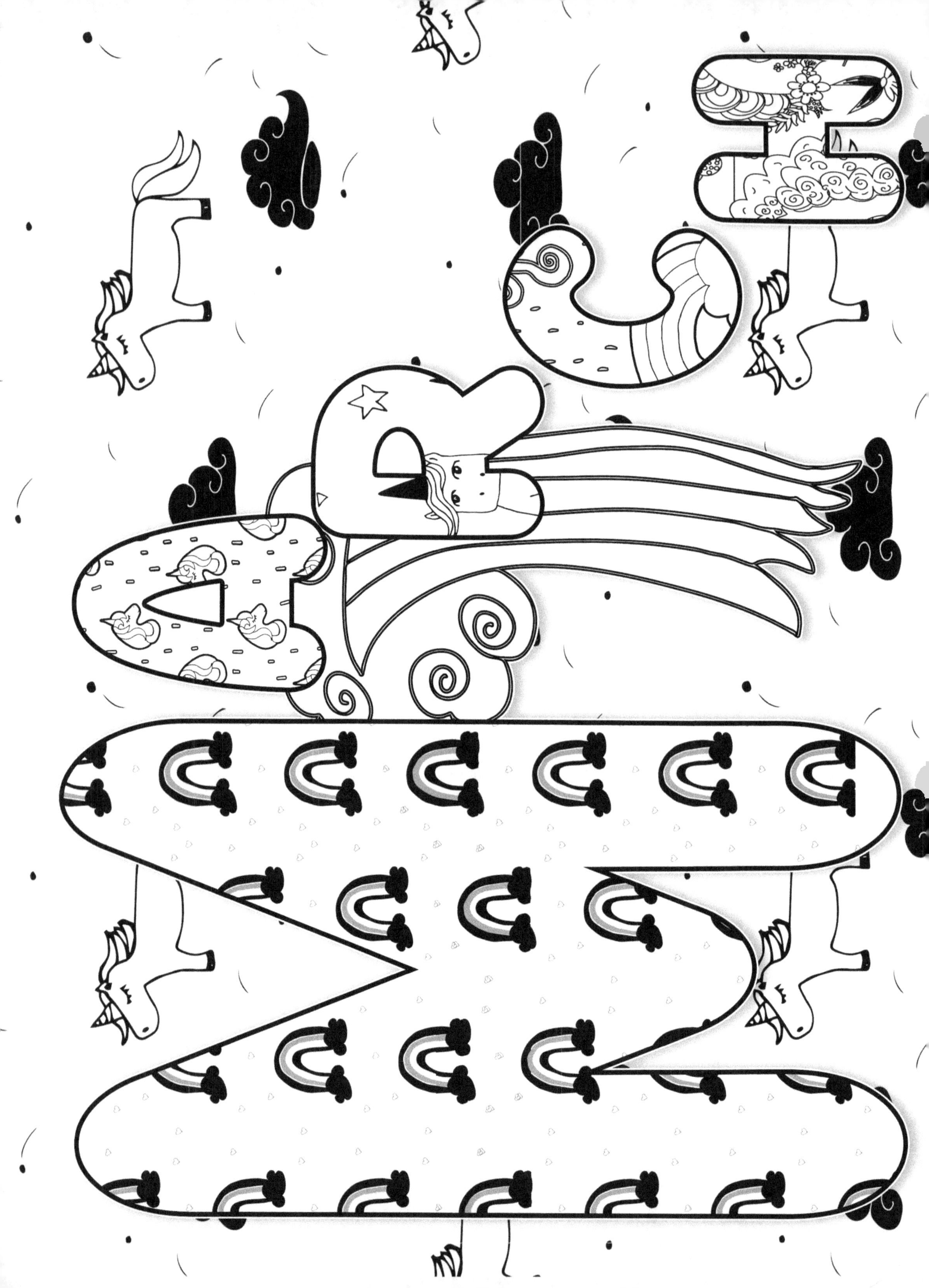

2020 2020

Sun.	Mon.	Tue.	Wed.	Thu.	Fri.	Sat.
1	2	3	4	5	6	7
8 Daylight Saving Time Begins	9	10	11	12	13	14
15	16	17 St. Patrick's Day	18	19	20	21
22	23	24	25	26	27	28
29	30	31				

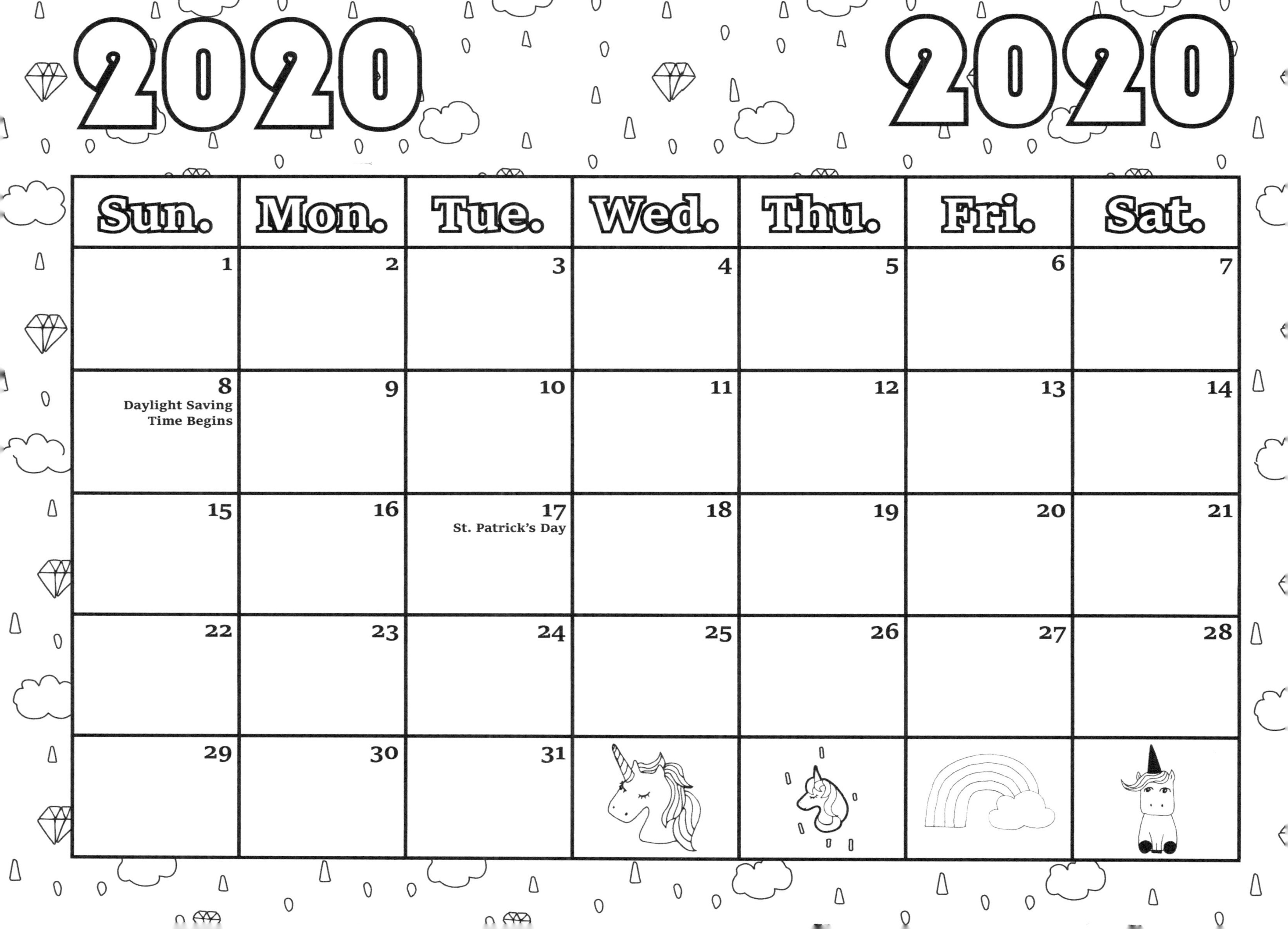

2020 2020

Sun.	Mon.	Tue.	Wed.	Thu.	Fri.	Sat.
			1	2	3	4
5	6	7	8	9	10	11
12 Easter	13	14	15	16	17	18
19	20	21	22	23	24	25
26	27	28	29	30		

2020 2020

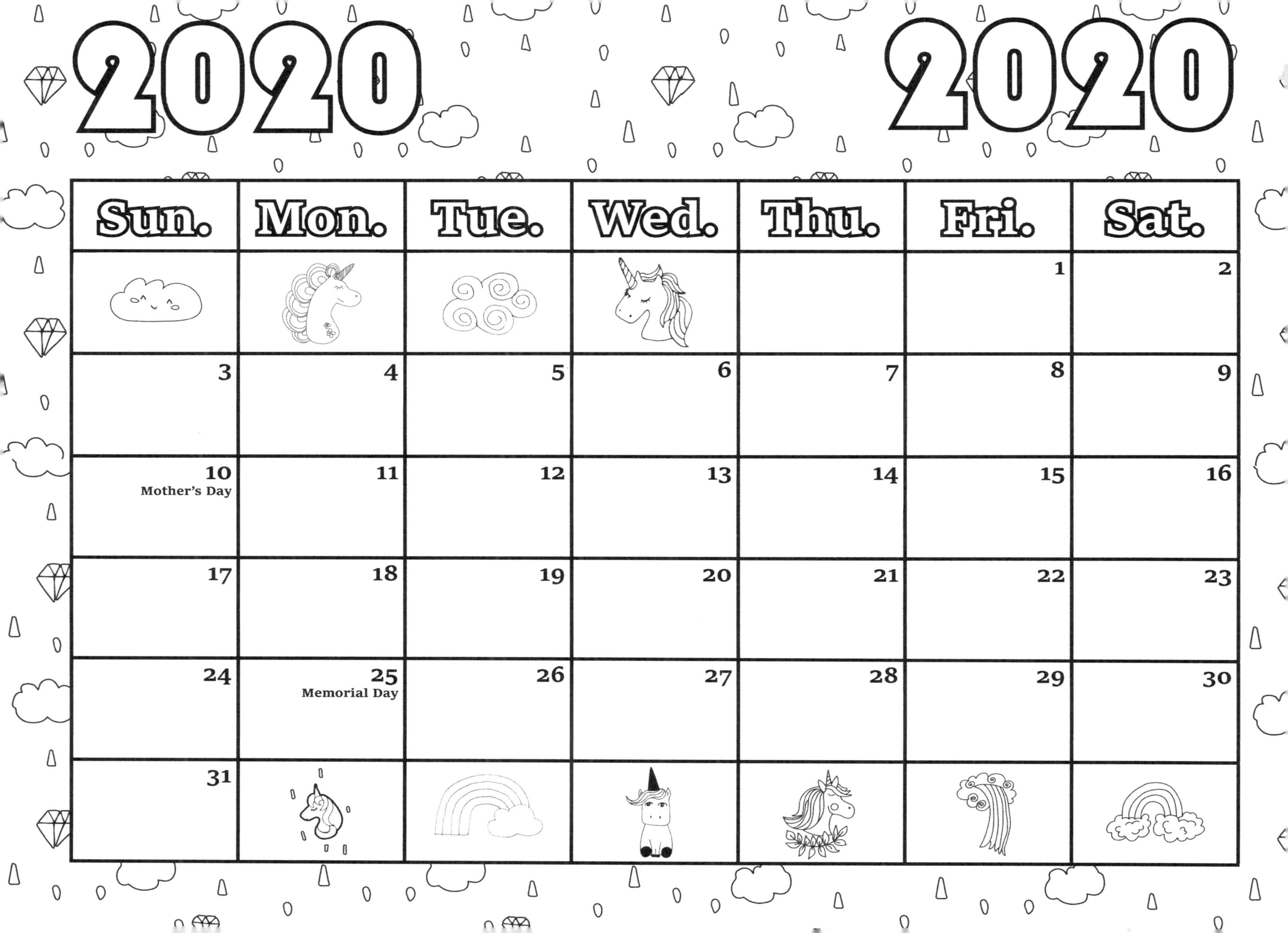

Sun.	Mon.	Tue.	Wed.	Thu.	Fri.	Sat.
					1	2
3	4	5	6	7	8	9
10 Mother's Day	11	12	13	14	15	16
17	18	19	20	21	22	23
24	25 Memorial Day	26	27	28	29	30
31						

2020 2020

Sun.	Mon.	Tue.	Wed.	Thu.	Fri.	Sat.
	1	2	3	4	5	6
7	8	9	10	11	12	13
14	15	16	17	18	19	20
21 Father's Day	22	23	24	25	26	27
28	29	30				

2020   2020

Sun.	Mon.	Tue.	Wed.	Thu.	Fri.	Sat.
			1	2	3 Independence Day Observed	4 Independence Day
5	6	7	8	9	10	11
12	13	14	15	16	17	18
19	20	21	22	23	24	25
26	27	28	29	30	31	

2020 2020

Sun.	Mon.	Tue.	Wed.	Thu.	Fri.	Sat.
						1
2	3	4	5	6	7	8
9	10	11	12	13	14	15
16	17	18	19	20	21	22
23	24	25	26	27	28	29
30	31					

2020 2020

Sun.	Mon.	Tue.	Wed.	Thu.	Fri.	Sat.
		1	2	3	4	5
6	7 Labor Day	8	9	10	11	12
13	14	15	16	17	18	19
20	21	22	23	24	25	26
27	28	29	30			

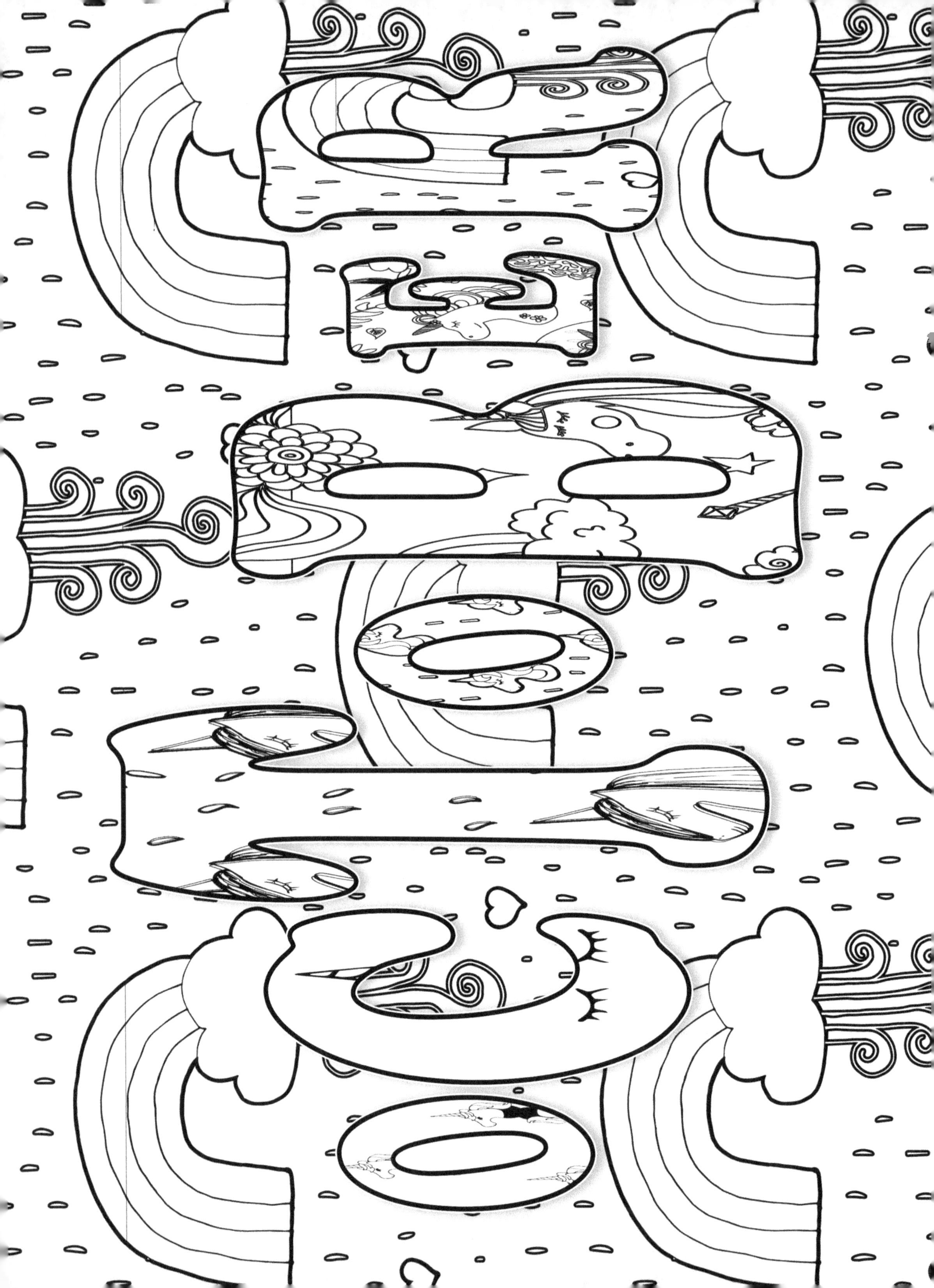

2020

Sun.	Mon.	Tue.	Wed.	Thu.	Fri.	Sat.
				1	2	3
4	5	6	7	8	9	10
11	12 Columbus Day	13	14	15	16	17
18	19	20	21	22	23	24
25	26	27	28	29	30	31 Halloween

2020   2020

Sun.	Mon.	Tue.	Wed.	Thu.	Fri.	Sat.
1 Daylight Saving Time Ends	2	3 Election Day	4	5	6	7
8	9	10	11 Veterans Day	12	13	14
15	16	17	18	19	20	21
22	23	24	25	26 Thanksgiving Day	27	28
29	30	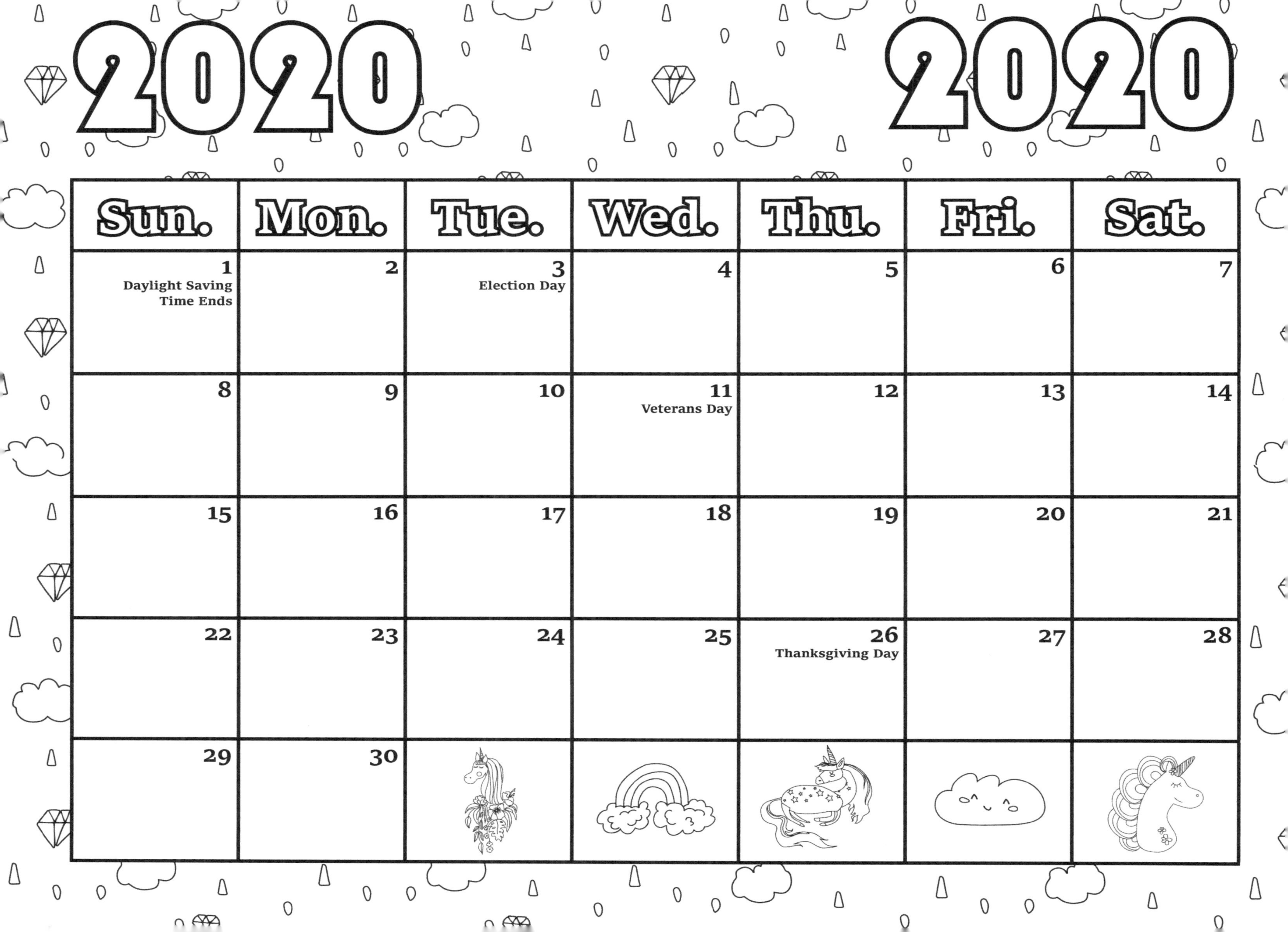				

2020 2020

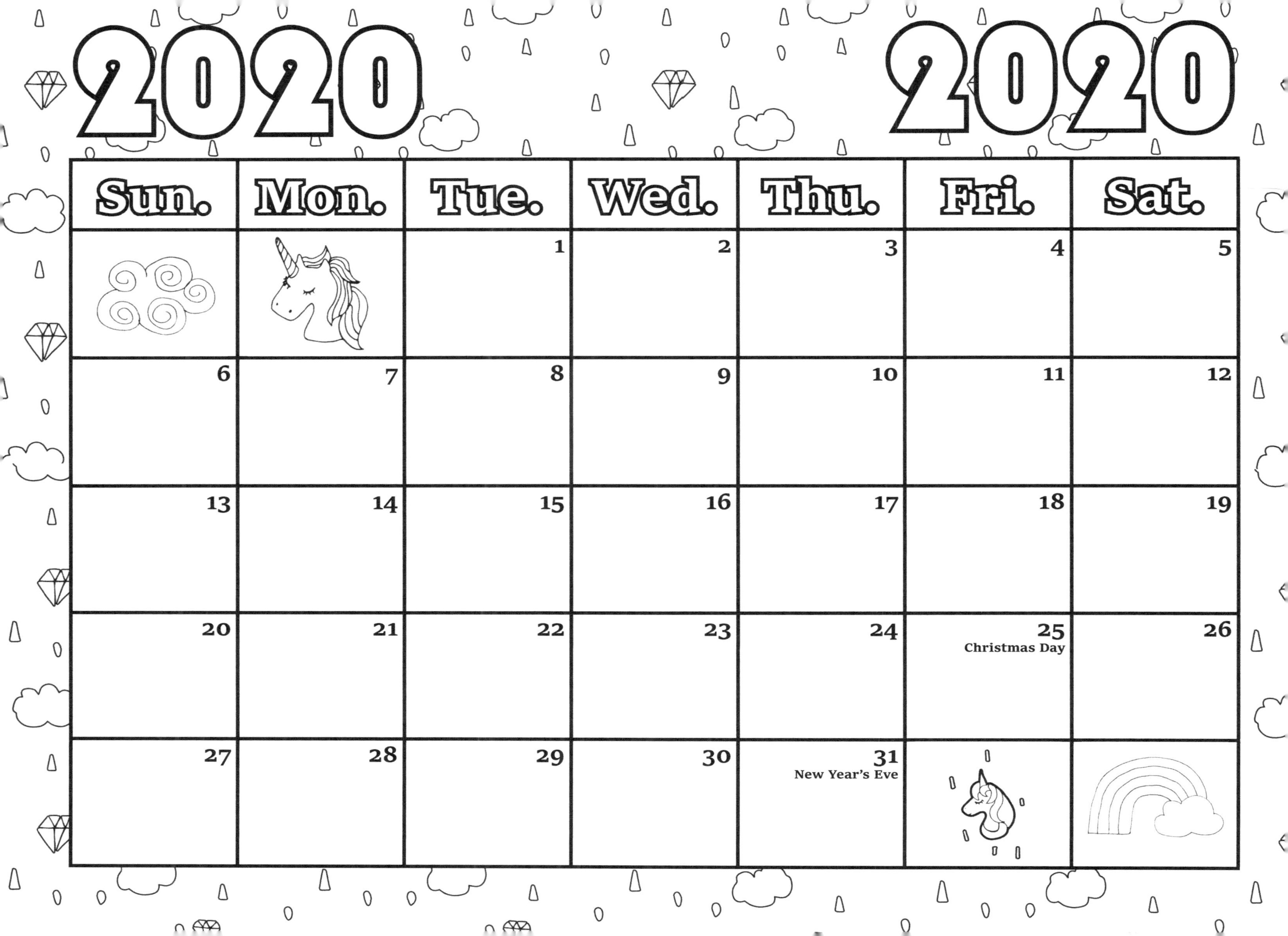

Sun.	Mon.	Tue.	Wed.	Thu.	Fri.	Sat.
			1	2	3	4
						5
6	7	8	9	10	11	12
13	14	15	16	17	18	19
20	21	22	23	24	25 Christmas Day	26
27	28	29	30	31 New Year's Eve		